SCAREDY-CAT
CATCHER

SCAREDY-CAT CATCHER

Betty Hicks

Illustrated by Adam McCauley

ROARING BROOK PRESS
NEW YORK

Many thanks to David Sherlin and Kenny Steed for their baseball expertise and for all the valuable contributions they made to the accuracy of this story. I am also grateful to Bailey Steed, a talented youth player, for reading the manuscript and liking it! —B. H.

Text copyright © 2009 by Betty Hicks
Illustrations copyright © 2009 by Adam McCauley

Published by Roaring Brook Press
Roaring Brook Press is a division of
Holtzbrinck Publishing Holdings Limited Partnership
175 Fifth Avenue, New York, New York 10010
www.roaringbrookpress.com

Cataloging-in-Publication Data is on file at the Library of Congress
ISBN-13: 978-1-59643-246-8
ISBN-10: 1-59643-246-2

Roaring Brook Press books are available for special promotions and premiums.
For details, contact: Director of Special Markets, Holtzbrinck Publishers.

Book design by Jennifer Browne
Printed in the United States of America
First Edition March 2009
2   4   6   8   10   9   7   5   3   1

For Jason

CONTENTS

THE TERRIBLE TAG

Rocky loved to play baseball. He was the best catcher in the league.

Whump!

The ball landed in his glove. Dead center. An easy catch.

In one motion, Rocky stepped onto the third-base line, leaned forward, and lowered his glove. He was ready to tag out the runner racing toward home plate.

The runner from third slid for home, kicking up dust and gravel. Two feet blasted into sight. The cleats aimed at Rocky.

The fans shouted, *"Tag-him-tag-him-tag-him!"*

Crack! Pain shot through Rocky's arm. Blazing pain. Rocky saw a dazzling white light. His arm—limp.

Then, his whole world turned to darkness, loaded with stars.

That's how Rocky's season had ended. But now, a whole year had passed since the runner from third had broken Rocky's arm. A new baseball season was ready to start.

Rocky smacked his fist into his catcher's mitt. No pain. Not even a twinge. He couldn't wait to play again.

"Hey! Batter-batter-batter!" taunted Rocky's teammates from the dugout. His team, the Pirates, was playing the Astros.

Rocky squatted behind the batter. He wore his mask, chest protector, and leg guards. He held up his catcher's mitt. Ready for the pitch.

"Batter-batter-batter-swing!"

The batter swung hard at Henry's fastball.

Whoosh! Nothing but air.

Rocky caught it.

"Strike three!" called the umpire. He flipped his thumb up and away. "You're out!"

Rocky zinged the ball back to Henry on the pitcher's mound.

He couldn't help smiling—he was so happy to be playing ball again.

The next batter swung hard.

Crack!

The ball sailed deep into left field. The left fielder dropped the catch!

The runner crossed first base and streaked toward second.

The left fielder scrambled to pick up the ball. He bobbled it. The runner rounded second.

"Throw to third!" shouted Rocky's coach. The throw went wide. So wide, the third baseman lunged away from the base to catch it. Rocky watched the runner tag third and head for home.

He's crazy! thought Rocky. He'll never make it. I can tag him out so easy.

The third baseman hurled the ball, straight to Rocky.

Rocky reached forward. Ready.

Whump! He caught it.

Two legs slid toward Rocky. Gravel flying. Cleats coming at him.

The fans shouted, *"Tag-him-tag-him-tag-him!"*

Rocky jerked his arm out of the way.

"Safe!" cried the umpire.

Rocky stared at his glove.

The Pirates' fans groaned.

What had Rocky done?

BUGS ON THE BRAIN

Rocky sat, slouched over, on the curb in front of Rita's house.

He wasn't the best player in the league anymore. He was the worst.

The Astros had beaten the Pirates. They'd scored three more runs, and Rocky should have stopped every one of them.

But he hadn't.

All of a sudden, he couldn't tag out a flea.

But, *why?*

"Relax," urged Henry.

"You'll be fine," soothed Rita.

"It's one of those can't-help-it things," explained Jazz. She creeped her fingers across the top of her head. "Bugs on the brain. You know—it's all in your head."

"*What's* all in my head?" groaned Rocky.

"Fear," said Jazz. "You're afraid."

"Of breaking your arm again," added Henry.

"Oh, great," muttered Rocky. "So how do I get bugs *off* my brain?"

"Here," said Goose, yanking on something stuck in his pocket. Out popped a red Tootsie Pop—without its wrapper.

Chops, Rocky's bulldog, sniffed the air.

The lollipop was covered with fuzzy gray lint.

"Eeew," said Rita.

"No thanks." Rocky shook his head. He didn't feel like eating anything.

Henry, Rita, Jazz, and Goose were Rocky's friends. They all lived in the same neighborhood. Five friends. Exactly enough for a basketball team. Or for any other sport they wanted to play. Rocky knew he was lucky—except for this bugs-on-the-brain thing.

Last year he'd been a catcher who would have made the all-star team—if he hadn't gotten hurt. Now he was a wimp who couldn't protect home plate from a house fly.

But he wouldn't quit. Rocky never quit.

When he was only two, he'd climbed to the top of the tallest lighthouse in America with his parents. "Don't help me. I can do it," he'd gasped. And he did do it. All 269 steps. When he reached the top, he pumped his fists in the air and danced.

That's when his parents nicknamed him Rocky—after the boxer in the movie—the one who trained by climbing steps and who never gave up.

Rocky *would* fix his problem. But how?

"I think," said Henry, poking his own chest with his thumb, "you just need to play again."

"Yeah," said Goose. "Next game, you'll be your old self."

Rita and Jazz smiled and nodded.

Rocky hoped they were right.

7

DOUBLE PLAY

The Pirates were playing the Cubs.

So far, the Pirates were winning. But Rocky was worried. Not about breaking his arm. No, he was afraid of messing up again.

Before the game, Jazz had said, "Think positive. Tell yourself you can do it."

"Because you *can* do it," added Henry.

Yes, thought Rocky. I can.

Rocky was small, but he had a good arm. He could nail the second baseman, all the way from home plate.

And he was smart. He knew what pitch to signal. And how to crouch and stand up fast—ready to throw if a runner tried to steal a base.

But could he tag a runner out at home plate?

Yes. Of course, he could.

It was the bottom of the final inning. Rocky's team,

the Pirates, led the Cubs, three to two. Both of the Cubs' runs had been home runs—no chance to tag anyone out.

A Cub stood on second base. Another one on third. Both of them were tensed and ready to run.

Only one out.

Rocky remembered Jazz's advice. *I'm good*, he told himself. *I can do this.* He had been telling himself that the whole game.

Suddenly, Rocky heard loud music playing inside his head. It was the kind that boomed in movies when the good guy was about to get shoved off a cliff.

What if he blew it?

Rocky squeezed his eyes shut. He crossed his fingers and made a wish. *Two more strikeouts, Henry. Please.*

A fresh batter stepped up to the plate.

Rocky pointed one finger down—the signal for Henry to pitch another fastball.

Henry nodded. He touched the brim of his cap. Henry always touched the brim of his cap. For luck.

Strike him out. Rocky moved his lips silently.

"Hey! Batter-batter-batter," chanted the Pirates, trying to break the batter's focus. To mess with his head. To make him swing at a bad throw.

The pitch zipped across home plate.

Smack!

A line drive streaked past the first baseman. It bounced into right field. Goose scooped it up and threw it to first base.

Two outs!

But the runner on third had already crossed home plate. *Game tied!*

The Cub on second was headed for home—the winning run!

Zing! The first baseman whipped the ball straight to Rocky.

Double play, thought Rocky. *I can do it.*

The Cub slid toward home plate.

The ball smacked into Rocky's glove. *Tag him!*

Rocky lowered his glove. Then—as if he'd touched fire—he yanked it away from the runner.

"*Safe!*" signaled the umpire.

Rocky couldn't believe it! They'd lost the game. No. *He'd* lost the game.

He'd been confident. He'd tried not to flinch. Why couldn't he do this? He wasn't a wimp. He wasn't!

Rocky saw the surprise on the faces of his teammates.

Their star catcher! A wuss.

DIRTY ROTTEN REFLEX

Rocky sagged on his back steps with Chops. He buried his face in his hands.

The Pirates had lost, and it was his fault.

"My problem is *not* in my head!" he shouted at his friends. "It's in my arm!"

"Yeah," said Rita. "So. We'll just have to fix your arm."

"Easy for you to say," said Rocky.

"All you need is practice," said Goose.

"Yes!" exclaimed Henry. "Remember when Goose was a crummy goalie—"

"I was never crummy," said Goose.

"—and we all helped him practice until he was good?"

Rocky did remember. Goose had worked hard. They all helped him. And, it worked!

"You have to unlearn your muscle jerk," said Jazz. "It's become a reflex."

"Huh?" said Rocky. Jazz read a lot. And sometimes used big words. She knew stuff.

"A *reflex*," she repeated. "It's when you can't help it. Like if you touch a hot burner on the stove, your hand jerks away. Your body acts without asking your brain."

"I have a dirty, rotten reflex," moaned Rocky. He eyed Jazz hopefully. "Can you fix it?"

"*We* can fix it," said Henry, excited. "I'll throw to Rocky. Goose, you slide toward him. Rita, you're the umpire. Jazz, you be coach."

"Cool," said Goose.

Rita clapped her hands and twirled.

Jazz made a fist and punched the air.

"We'll practice for as long as it takes," said Henry. "Until Rocky keeps his glove down." Henry paused. He chuckled. "Or until Goose's legs get too bloody."

Goose's goofball grin spread across his face. He loved to slide. He collected scabs.

THE SCAB CURE

This isn't working, thought Rocky.

Every time Goose slid, Rocky jerked back his arm too soon.

Jazz kept shouting, "Don't give up! You can do this!"

Rocky would *never* give up. But his friends looked unhappy. Worn out. Even Goose, who loved to slide, seemed tired.

"One more time," said Jazz.

Rocky cleared his head. *Focus!* he told himself. *Keep your glove in front of the plate.*

Rocky tried to do all the things he'd learned from his coach. Stand in front of the plate. Make the tag. Then get your arm out of the way. Quick. It made sense to Rocky's brain, but his arm wasn't listening.

Rocky snagged the throw from Henry. He turned

and put his glove exactly where Coach had taught him. Goose's cleats came at him—but not as fast as before.

"You're out!" Rita screamed at Goose. She did a wiggle dance with her hips.

"Really?" Rocky was surprised. Had he actually tagged Goose out, or was Rita just being nice?

Goose hopped up off the ground and high-fived him.

Henry ran over and slapped his back so hard, Rocky thought his teeth might pop loose.

"Again!" shouted Jazz. "Do it again!"

Rocky knew Goose had slowed down. Was that why he hadn't flinched?

But Goose wasn't tired anymore. He was hyped. Loaded with fresh energy. Ready to mow Rocky down.

Rocky caught the throw. He stepped on the baseline. His glove blocked the path to home plate.

Goose came at him like a freight train. Smoking. Flying. Spewing tiny rocks and grinding dirt.

Rocky closed his eyes. This time he felt his glove make contact. He knew it did.

"Out!" yelled Rita.

Rocky had done it! Twice. He could do it again.
And again. He knew he could.

His next game was two days away. Rocky couldn't
wait!

THE TERRIBLE TRUTH

When Rocky arrived at his next game, he felt great! Ready to play!

Two players from the other team pointed at him. *"Scaredy-cat catcher!"* they jeered.

Rocky's face flamed red. The Cubs must have told everyone he was a wimp.

He balled up his fists and kept walking.

Who calls people *scaredy-cats*, anyway? Babies, that's who. Five-year-olds.

Rocky was *not* scared.

He was cured!

Rocky's team batted first. They scored four runs in eight minutes.

When the opposing team, the Rangers, stepped up to the plate, Henry struck out the first three batters. One. Two. Three. Just like that. This game was going to be easy. Rocky began to worry he wouldn't get to show that he could tag out a runner.

His chance came in the fifth inning. The Rangers still hadn't scored, but they had a runner on second base. The batter hit a high ball into center field.

An easy out, thought Rocky.

But the Pirate dropped it. The Ranger on second rounded third and streaked for home.

Rocky stood ready.

"Hit your cutoff!" yelled Coach to the infield. Rocky's teammates relayed the throw to home.

Rocky had to stretch to catch it, but he snagged it.

He turned and reached low to tag the runner. Rocky heard the sound of grinding dirt. He saw the runner's legs sliding at him fast.

A chant exploded from the Rangers' dugout: *"Scaredy-cat-scaredy-cat-scaredy-cat."*

Suddenly another sound exploded in Rocky's head. *Crack!* The memory of his arm breaking.

Rocky jerked back his glove.

"Safe!" called the umpire.

The Pirates still won. But Rocky felt worse than slime.

After the game, Goose elbowed Rocky's arm. "Too bad," he said.

"Hang in there," added Henry. "We'll keep practicing."

Coach strolled over and rumpled Rocky's hair.
"Let's talk."

Rocky plodded behind Coach until they were out
of earshot of the team. Coach put his hand on
Rocky's shoulder.

"A runner should be going for the base—not for
you," said Coach. "The kid who broke your arm was
out of control."

Rocky knew that. But if it had happened once, it
could happen again.

"When I was your age," said Coach, "I got hit in the
head with a pitched ball. Knocked me out. Months
went by before I could stand close to home plate
again."

Rocky felt a tingly swell in his chest. It had happened to Coach, too! Maybe Rocky wasn't a wuss.

But he didn't *have* months. He needed to play well
now. When the regular season was over, Rocky
wanted to make the all-star team. The way he should
have last year.

"Thanks, Coach," Rocky mumbled. "I'll keep trying."

"Rocky," said Coach, smiling, "you're not a good catcher . . ."

Rocky lowered his head.

"You're a *great* catcher."

Rocky's head jerked back up. "Really?"

Yes! he thought. *But . . . but . . .* His brain began to stutter. *Why can't I tag out a runner?*

Suddenly Rocky knew the truth. The terrible truth.

He was afraid of pain. He *was* a scaredy-cat.

And nothing he or his friends could do would ever change that fact.

THE RIGHT THING

Rocky's bulldog, Chops, pushed his head onto Rocky's lap. His jowls melted over Rocky's leg like two slabs of soft butter. Rocky sat up straighter and scratched Chops behind one ear.

Chops rolled his eyes up at Rocky—warm, happy eyes that said, *Rocky, you're great.* Rocky was glad Chops didn't know the truth—that he was never going to keep his glove down.

Because he was afraid.

Yes, he *had* learned to keep his arm down in practice. But it was *Goose—his friend—*sliding toward him. Even when Goose came at him fast, Rocky knew Goose would never break his arm.

For the first time in his life, Rocky thought about quitting. Even though he never gave up. Not ever.

But what choice did he have? Sticking with baseball was hurting his team.

Quitting was the right thing to do.

Rocky rubbed Chops's ear. He forced a smile and said, "I'll have more time to play with you, now."

Chops wagged his tail.

Rocky noticed his skateboard, flipped upside down in the driveway. Maybe he could teach Chops to ride a skateboard.

Rocky had seen a video of a dog that could do it. He would put his front paw on the board. Then he'd run along, push with his other three legs, and hop on. The dog had shot down the street like a bullet.

Rocky got up and turned his skateboard over. He placed Chops on top of the board.

Chops hopped off. He wagged his tail.

"No." Rocky put him back on again. "Stay!"

Chops cocked his head. *Why?*

Slowly, Rocky rolled the skateboard back and forth. Chops dug in his claws and hung on.

"Hang ten," said Rocky. Not that Chops *could* hang ten. That was a tricky move a skateboarder did when his feet hugged the front of the board. But Rocky thought it made an awesome dog command.

"Hey!" called Goose, walking down Rocky's drive-way. "What's up?"

"I'm teaching Chops to skateboard."

"Cool," said Goose.

As Rocky rolled Chops back and forth, Rita, Jazz, and Henry showed up.

They all cheered as Chops held on. Then, Chops hopped off and jumped up on everyone's shins. He licked Henry's knee.

Henry tossed a baseball up in the air and caught it. "Ready for practice?" he asked.

Rocky studied his feet. How would he tell his friends he was quitting baseball?

"Not today," he mumbled.

"How come?" asked Goose.

"My arm's sore," Rocky lied. "The doctor said if it ever hurt, to give it a rest." That part was true.

"It's been healed for months!" said Rita.

Rocky's face flushed pink.

Jazz stared at him. "You're giving up, aren't you?"

"What?" Henry's jaw dropped. "No way! Rocky never quits. Go on. Tell her," urged Henry. "Tell Jazz you never quit!"

Rocky squeezed his hands into fists. He bit his bottom lip. He wanted to say that he wasn't quitting. But he couldn't.

SPITTING LIKE A PRO

"That's crazy!" "Don't quit." "You can do it." "We'll help you."

Rocky's friends fired words at him like fast balls. Words to change Rocky's mind.

"I don't *want* to quit," argued Rocky. "I *have* to. For the team."

"One more game," said Henry. "Try one more time."

Rocky wanted to try, but what if he really was a scaredy-cat? What if he made the Pirates lose? He shook his head. No.

Henry was so upset, he spit. *Splat.* Right on Rocky's driveway.

"Eeew," said Rita.

Goose laughed. He coughed up some phlegm and hocked it six feet. It landed in a red tulip. Goose could spit better than anybody.

"This isn't funny, Goose!" said Henry.

"Sorry," said Goose. He hunched his shoulders and stuffed his hands into his pockets. Then, suddenly, he flashed an excited look at Henry.

"Rocky," said Goose. "I bet I can hit that tulip again."

Rocky shrugged. Usually he thought spitting was cool, but right now he didn't care.

"Look," said Goose. I can even hit *that* tulip." He pointed to a yellow tulip *ten* feet away.

Rocky glanced at the flower. "No way," he muttered.

"Wanna bet?" said Goose.

Rocky shrugged again. "Sure."

"Here's the deal," said Goose, chopping the air with one hand. "If I hit the tulip, you have to play one more baseball game." He paused and looked Rocky in the eye. "If I miss, you get to quit."

All of Rocky's friends looked at him, waiting for an answer.

A flutter ran through Rocky's gut. He didn't think he could stand it if he cost the Pirates another game. He stared at the yellow tulip. Goose could spit like a pro. No doubt about it. But that flower was a long way off. Was Goose *that* good?

"It's a bet," said Rocky.

Henry grinned. Rita clapped. Jazz held her breath.

Goose held his thumb out in front of one eye. Setting his aim. He threw his head back, then *"Pluuh!"* He let one rip.

Plop! The glob dropped into the yellow tulip.

Henry and Jazz high-fived Goose. Rita shouted, *"Woo-hoo!"*

Rocky was surprised to hear happy music playing inside his head. He had the best friends on the whole planet.

Rocky spent the rest of the afternoon coaxing Chops onto the skateboard.

Every time Chops hopped onto it by himself, Rocky handed him a treat.

"Good dog," he praised.

Then he smiled to himself and thought, *If my friends want me to play baseball, I will. I won't let them down.*

WHO BUNTS?

Two days later, the Pirates played the Reds.

Rocky's chance came in the third inning. With one out and runners on second and third.

Henry had thrown seven fastballs in a row. Rocky thought it was time for a switch. He signaled Henry to throw a changeup.

Henry nodded. He spit. He touched the brim of his cap.

Rocky wanted to spit, too, but he had a mask on. He was afraid it might hit the mask and dribble down his chin.

Henry's pitch went wide. Rocky caught it.

Ball one.

"Batter-batter-batter!" chanted the Pirates from the dugout.

A swing and a miss.

The count was one ball, one strike. The next pitch was right in the middle of the strike zone.

The batter bunted! *What?* Who tells a batter to bunt with a runner on second and third?

A coach who knew Rocky couldn't tag out a flea, that's who!

Henry dove forward and scooped up the ball. He pitched it to Rocky to stop the run.

Rocky caught it.

"Scaredy-cat-scaredy-cat-scaredy-cat!" chanted the Reds.

Rocky flinched. Then he turned. Lowered his glove. And kept it down. He didn't care if both arms broke. He'd show them!

Blap! The runner's foot struck home plate.

"Safe!" signaled the umpire.

Safe? Rocky couldn't believe it! He'd kept his glove low. He hadn't been scared. He'd tagged him out. Hadn't he?

Rocky looked down at his feet. He was standing *behind* the base. Exactly where he shouldn't be.

He couldn't tag out a gnat from there.

He was sure he'd moved forward of the base. But his feet didn't lie. Neither did the faces of his teammates.

All of them were trying to hide looks that said, *Rocky, you blew it.* Again.

Rocky asked Coach to take him out of the game.

He told him his arm hurt where he'd broken it.

HANG TEN

For a week, Rocky sat on the bench.

"Let me know when you're ready to play," said Coach.

Ha! thought Rocky. He would never be ready.

Nothing worked. Believing in himself had failed. Practicing hadn't worked. After all, practice wasn't a *real* game. Something about the real thing messed with Rocky's mind.

Was it the chanting? *Scaredy-cat-scaredy-cat-scaredy-cat.*

Well . . . what could Rocky do about that?

Nothing.

He pictured himself sneaking into the other team's dugout. Slapping duct tape over everyone's mouth.

Dumb idea.

All week, Coach played someone else as catcher.

The only good thing in Rocky's life was Chops.

Chops was turning into a skateboarding wizard. Every day, Rocky spent time with him. Teaching him. Training him. *At least* he *can learn*, thought Rocky.

Rocky pulled his skateboard out from under his bed. Chops's tail wagged as if it had a motor. He jumped up on Rocky's legs. He spun around the bedroom in a tight circle.

So far, Chops had skateboarded only in Rocky's driveway. Today, Rocky decided to take him to the parking lot of Murray Middle School. It was only four blocks away. That way, Chops would have more space. He could to learn how to turn.

Chops was so excited, Rocky worried he'd have a heart attack. All the way to the school, Chops strained at his leash.

As soon as Rocky put

down the board, Chops put one paw on it. He began to run with his other three legs.

"Hang ten!" yelled Rocky.

Chops hopped on and took off across the parking lot. His ears spread out like wings. He could go straight forever.

The board banged into the curb, and Chops hopped off. He put his paw back on it. He pushed with his legs and jumped on again.

He sailed straight back to Rocky. Chops looked as if he were grinning.

"Good boy!" exclaimed Rocky, hugging him. He gave Chops a doggie treat. Then he shouted, "Hang ten!" and Chops took off again.

This time he headed a new way. Rocky spotted a break in the curb. It led down a steep paved driveway beside the building. Chops headed straight for it.

"No!" shouted Rocky. "Stop! Turn! Jump!"

Chops hadn't learned any of those commands.

Rocky watched Chops plunge out of sight. He ran.

Blam!

Rocky stopped at the top of the tall hill and looked down. Metal trash cans lay overturned at the bottom. The skateboard was upside down, its wheels still spinning.

Chops was sprawled out next to it.

He wasn't moving.

11

SHOTS, NEEDLES, AND FEAR

Rocky held Chops in his lap all the way to the animal clinic.

If Chops moved—even one inch—he whimpered.

"Drive faster," Rocky told his mom.

Mom reached over and stroked Chops's head. Then she squeezed Rocky's arm. "He's going to be fine," she said. But her voice was small and squeaky.

She's scared, thought Rocky. He bit his lip and hoped he wouldn't cry.

The air inside the animal clinic felt cold. To Rocky, it smelled like shots and needles.

And fear.

This time, the music in Rocky's head sounded like a drum. Thumping with his heartbeat. No tune. Just noisy thuds.

He handed Chops to a woman in a white coat who hurried forward.

"Fix him," Rocky whispered. "Please."

"Don't you worry," she answered. Then she whisked Chops away through two swinging doors.

But Rocky *did* worry. And he waited.

And he told himself he didn't deserve a dog like Chops.

And then he waited some more.

It seemed like hours before the doctor came back. She carried Chops. He looked limp and broken, but his tail wagged when he spotted Rocky.

"Chops has two cracked ribs," said the doctor. "There's no way to put a cast on them. Just keep him still, and he'll be fine before you know it."

Trumpets rang out inside Rocky's head. *He'll be fine!* Rocky felt lighter—as if he'd been turned into a balloon.

Then he froze.

Keep Chops still? Tell him not to move?

That would be like telling school not to start.

No way.

Rocky had no choice: he had to keep Chops in a cage. He listened to him bark and whine. He tried to ignore his super-sad eyes that asked, *Why are you being so mean?*

At least Rocky wasn't going to baseball practice anymore. He could take care of Chops.

After a week, the doctor said Chops could leave his

cage. He could walk around—some. No running. No jumping.

And no skateboarding! thought Rocky. Ha! As if Chops would ever want to skateboard again.

Rocky opened the dog cage. Chops jumped up on Rocky's leg. He licked his knee.

"No!" scolded Rocky. He reached down and hugged Chops gently. He petted him and said, "I'm so sorry. No jumping. You just can't."

Chops trotted over and sniffed under Rocky's bed. The motor in his tail revved up. He tugged on the skateboard with his teeth. He eased it out and hopped on. His face tilted up toward Rocky's. It said, *Can I, huh? Please. Please. Can I?*

CRAZY DOG? SUPER DOG!

Jazz sat beside Rocky on the curb. She'd brought Chops a new chew toy.

Rocky and Jazz watched Chops sprawl on the grass and gnaw his get-well present.

"How's he doing?" asked Jazz.

"Good," answered Rocky. "Almost healed . . . but crazy."

"*Crazy?*"

"Yeah," said Rocky. "*Wham! Blap!* The goofy dog wipes out. Cracks two ribs. He could've been killed. And guess what?"

"What?"

"He still wants to ride my skateboard."

"No," said Jazz.

"Yes," answered Rocky.

"He *is* crazy," said Jazz.

42

"Yeah," said Rocky. But he knew he didn't mean it. Secretly, he thought Chops was a hero.

Jazz looked at Chops. She thought for a minute. "Actually, I think he's brave," she said.

Rocky felt a warm glow swell inside his chest. Neither of them spoke for a while. They just watched Chops. Like he was their own private TV show—*A Day in the Life of Super Dog*.

"After a deadly drop from a thousand feet," Rocky made his voice sound like a newscaster, "Super Dog survives!"

"Yeah." Jazz giggled. "He rests. He chews. He slimes the grass with drool. Then . . . suddenly . . . he leaps up! Ready to dive into the jaws of danger."

"And stomp out evil."

"He's *not* leaping up," said Jazz, waiting for Chops to do what she'd said.

"Why can't *I* do that?" asked Rocky.

"Leap up?"

"No," said Rocky. "Dive into the jaws of danger."

"Tell Coach you'll play again," said Jazz.

Rocky grabbed a clump of grass and twisted it until pieces tore off in his hand.

"I can tag Goose out—in practice," he said. "But not when it really counts."

He threw the blades onto the pavement and ground them with his foot. "Or when people yell *scaredy-cat*."

"The chanting," said Jazz. "It breaks your focus."

"Well, duh," said Rocky.

Jazz thought a minute. "It reminds you of what you're afraid of."

"Double duh," said Rocky.

Jazz ignored him. "You need something to zap your

focus back." What had Jazz been reading now? *Don't Be Mental? How to Be a Brain Doctor?*

"I've got it!" shrieked Jazz. She jumped up so fast, Chops dropped his chew toy.

"Got what?" asked Rocky.

"The best idea in the history of the world," said Jazz. "Next game—tomorrow—you tell Coach you're ready. Leave the rest to me."

"I don't know," said Rocky, shaking his head. "What're you thinking?"

"If I told you," said Jazz, "it wouldn't work."

DEVIL RAYS RULE!

Rocky barely slept a wink all night. Every time he closed his eyes, they popped open again. What *was* Jazz's idea?

The next morning in class, he couldn't focus on his schoolwork. So he drew a tattoo on his arm. Of a pirate. Just like the logo on his baseball cap.

After school, he arrived early for his game. "Coach," said Rocky. "I'm ready. Can I play? Please."

Coach studied Rocky's face as if it were a jigsaw puzzle. "You sure?"

Was Rocky sure? No. But he said yes anyway.

"Great," said Coach, patting him on the back. "You're in."

Rocky gulped. Jazz's idea had better be good.

The game was close. The Pirates played the Devil Rays—the best team in the league. The Devil Rays ruled.

Neither team had gotten many hits.

Henry touched his cap for luck and fired fastballs. *Strike! Strike! Strike!* Rocky caught them and zinged them back.

Jazz kept winking at Rocky from the bleachers. What *was* her idea? Rita sat next to Jazz and shouted, "Rocky! Rocky! You the man!"

The score was zero to zero until the fourth inning.

On Henry's turn at bat, he got a base hit. Then Goose stepped up to the plate and knocked the ball out of the park! A home run!

Pirates, two. Devil Rays, zero.

In the next inning, the Devil Rays had runners on first and third. The runner on first stepped away from the base. He moved even farther. He was itching to steal second base.

Rocky watched him. He signaled Henry.

Henry wound up his pitch. Instead of throwing to Rocky, he turned and zinged it to first. The runner dived back to safety. Too late. Out.

Henry nodded to Rocky. Rocky nodded back.

Henry's next pitch was a changeup.

Whack! The batter connected.

Rocky stood ready to catch the throw. *And* make the tag.

The shortstop zinged the ball to Rocky. A wild

throw. No way he could reach it. The runner crossed home plate standing up. Pumping his fist.

Pirates, two. Devil Rays, one. At least it wasn't Rocky's fault.

Henry struck out the next two batters.

In the top of the sixth—the last inning—three Pirates struck out.

Three up. Three down. Just like that.

The Pirates took the field for the last time. All they needed was three outs, and the game would be over. Henry stood on the pitcher's mound. Rocky squatted to catch.

Henry struck out the first two batters.

"Go Pirates!" shouted half the fans.

"Go Devil Rays!" shouted the other half.

"Hey-batter-batter-batter-Swing!" screamed the Pirates' dugout.

Henry started his windup. The batter shifted his weight to his back foot, and then stepped forward. *Crack!* He hit a line drive deep into left field.

He rounded first base and slid into second. *Safe!*

The next batter had two balls, two strikes. Then he

smacked a grounder straight up the first-base line. It looked like an easy out. Game over. Pirates would win.

But the ball took a crazy bounce. It sailed right through the first baseman's glove, as if it had a hole in it. *Safe!*

The first baseman recovered the ball, but the runner from second had already rounded third. Like a rocket, he streaked for home.

Rocky stood exactly where he knew should be. *Make the catch. Tag the runner. Win the game.*

Whomp! Rocky caught the ball. He lowered his glove.

Arm down. Keep it down. Focus.

Cleats—sharp—scary—came at him fast. Blasting down the baseline. Sliding. Screeching.

Devil Rays shouted, *"Scaredy-cat-scaredy-cat-scaredy-cat!"*

Rocky felt his arm jerk up. As if it didn't belong to him.

And then Jazz's scream broke through the crowd noise: *"Chops-can-do-it-Chops-can-do-it-Chops-can-do-it!"*

Rocky slammed his glove back down.

"Out!" shouted the umpire.

"Yay!" screamed the Pirates.

MAGIC SPELL

Rocky and all of his friends raced up the steep steps to the parking lot after the game. When they reached the top, they shouted the tune of the theme song from Rocky. Then they pumped their fists in the air.

"Rocky, you were awesome!" cheered Rita. She punched him in the arm.

Rocky rubbed his arm and grinned. "Thanks, Rita, but Jazz did it."

"Don't be a goofball," scoffed Jazz. "*You* did it." She pounded Rocky on his back.

"Hey!" cried Henry. "What did Coach say?"

Rocky laughed. "First he said, 'Great tag!' Then he asked, 'What the heck does *chop-ska-do-ee* mean?'"

Jazz's eyes lit up like sparklers. *"Chops can do it!"* she cried. "What did you tell him?"

"I said it was a magic spell—one that I can use anytime I need it. For curing brain bugs."

"Let's try it on Goose," said Henry.

Goose rolled his eyes.

"Coach asked me if the spell worked on all-stars," said Rocky.

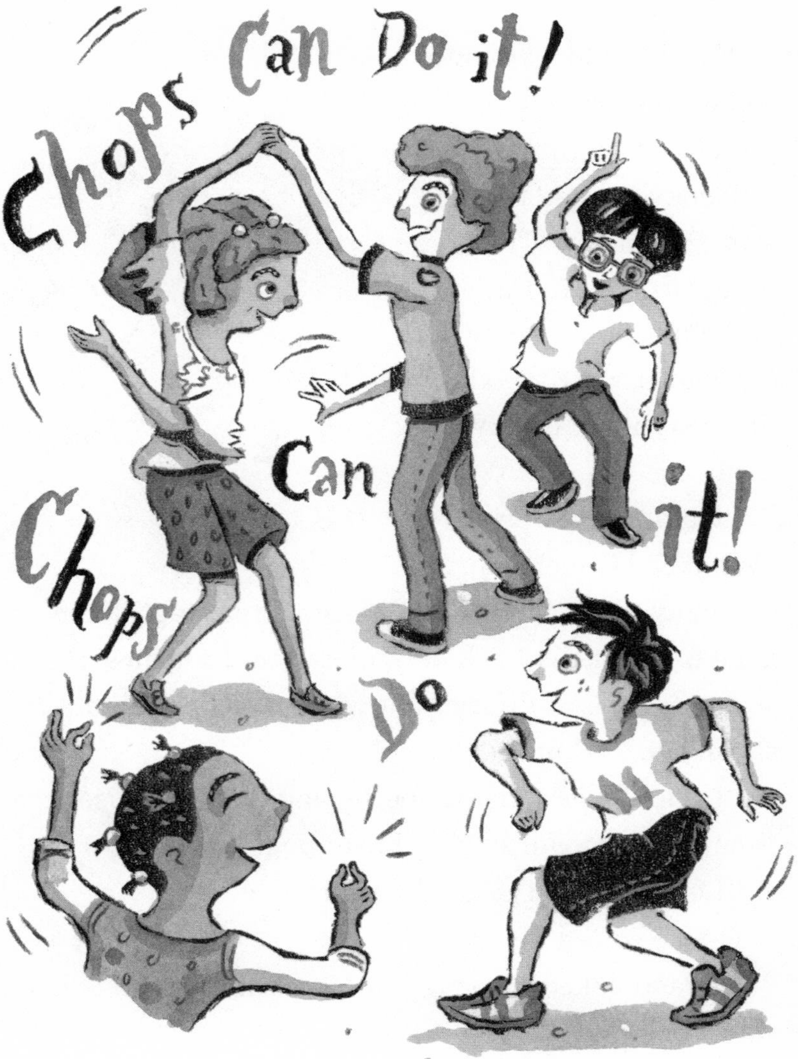
Chops Can Do it!
Chops Can Do it!

"You made *all-stars!*" cried Henry. He jerked Rocky's head into a headlock and rapped it with his knuckles.

"Would everybody please stop hitting me?" yelled Rocky. "I haven't made *all-stars*, yet." Rocky looked down to hide his smile. "But Coach said I was back in the running."

"You'll make it!" exclaimed Jazz.

Rocky stopped trying to hide his smile. He felt great. He had quit. But he had come back.

Rita began to dance, twirling and spinning.

Rocky circled his arms in time to her beat. *"Chops-can-do-it-Chops-can-do-it!"* he sang.

Jazz snapped her fingers. Henry did the twist.

Goose grabbed Rita's hand and twirled her like a top.

"Chops can do it," Rocky repeated.

"And Rocky did it," sang everyone else.